For Chloe, Marissa and Douglas

A special thanks to Dr. Alan H. Katz for his superb technical support

Sam and Sid were twin sneakers. They were born in Max's Shoe Store where they grew and thrived. They ate together, played together, and loved each other very much.

When they were a size six, Max, the manager of the shoe store, picked them up and took them out of their play room, which was the storage room. He placed them on a stand in the front window of the store.

Sam and Sid were in awe – they couldn't believe what they saw when they looked through the glass. They saw a bright, shiny world full of people, cars, cats and even dogs. Their eyes opened wide.

Sam especially loved watching all the people who walked by. He thought they looked so strange since they didn't have laces, or leatherbacks, or protruding tongues like he and his brother had, and wore proudly. Sam thought he was the luckiest sneaker in the world to be given the privilege of a window seat and to enjoy each exciting day with Sid by his side.

One day a little boy named Ben and his mother walked into the store. Sam heard Ben say to his mother, "I want blue sneakers!" Ben's mother said, "No Ben, You need white sneakers, just like your classmates." Ben insisted on trying on blue sneakers, and then red sneakers, and then green sneakers, but none of them fit him.

Ben was getting frustrated and began to cry. "Mommy, I will never find sneakers that fit me!"

Ben's mother then spied Sam and Sid sitting comfortably in the store window. "Let's try those cute white sneakers," she told the store manager.

Max, the kindly manager said, "Oh, Sam and Sid are wonderful sneakers; they are twins." "Even better," said Ben's mother. Max brought Ben the sneakers hoping they would fit.

When Ben tried on Sam and Sid he smiled because they fit perfectly! "I'll take these sneakers!" exclaimed Ben.

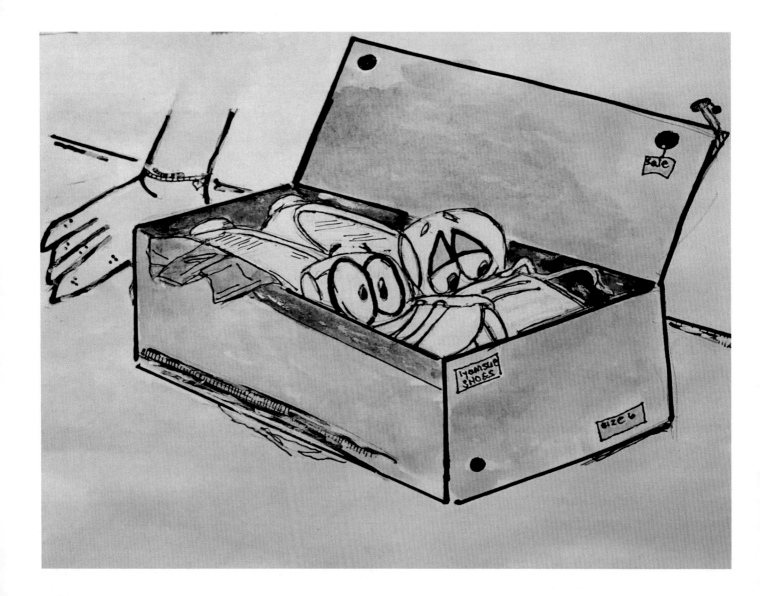

"Excellent!" said his mother, and they placed Sam and Sid in a box and took them home. Sam was not happy. He liked sitting in the store window, but Sid was excited for a new adventure.

When Ben arrived home, he quickly put on his new sneakers.

...And he joyfully ran outside to play. Sid enjoyed the feel of the moist grass under his back, but Sam the sneaker was upset and didn't like the dampness or texture of the grass. He wanted to be back on the store shelf. Sam wanted to feel comfortable, clean and dry.

Sam decided to do whatever he could to go back to the store. He wasn't going to cooperate and be a good sneaker.

Ben noticed that Sam, his right sneaker, began to be a problem. First, his right shoelace kept untying at the worst times. It untied when he was getting ready to leave for school and it also untied during his walk to school.

It untied when he was playing tag with friends

And it untied when he was
marching in the school band

Ben also noticed that he tripped a lot because he seemed to get little pebbles and small stones in his right sneaker.

Sometimes his sneaker seemed to fit poorly, and his heel would slip out of it.

Ben also noticed that his right sneaker was missing a lot of the time. When he woke up in the morning, Sid, his left sneaker, was always by his bed, but Sam was someplace else. Sometimes Sam was hidden under the bed.

Sometimes Sam was mixed in with Ben's toys that were scattered on the floor, and once Ben found Sam in the hamper under a pile of dirty clothes. Ben was confused and didn't know why his right sneaker wouldn't cooperate.

Sid felt sorry for Ben and told Sam to behave. "Ben is a really nice boy and he takes good care of us. You should appreciate Ben and be a good sneaker." Sam, replied, "*I am a good sneaker,* I just don't like it here; I miss the store and I miss Max!" Sid remarked, "Ben is wonderful and caring, be nice to him, he even cleaned us so well last night that we sparkle!"

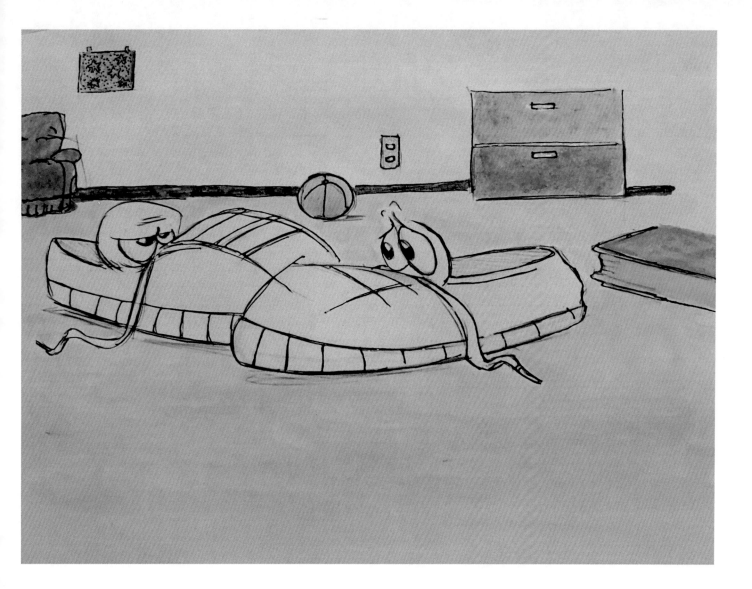

Sam kept acting ornery and didn't listen to Sid. His shoelaces were getting worn and frayed from constantly being untied. He wouldn't admit it but he was getting tired of doing the opposite of what a proper sneaker was supposed to do.

Then one day Sam reluctantly went to Ben's baseball game. 'I don't want to be here," he whined. Sid replied, "You need to be here; we have to help Ben win the game. Be a team player and support Ben!" Sam thought about what Sid said and still felt unsure whether or not he was going to help Ben play his best.

Sam and Sid giggled as they felt Ben's toes wiggle excitedly. They waited for what seemed like a long time, but soon the game began. The pitchers were pitching, the batters were batting, and the fielders were fielding. By the ninth inning the score was tied and the crowd was roaring. Ben was up and he approached the plate. He gripped the bat and he watched the ball come closer and closer.

Ben was nervous, but he kept his eyes on the ball and then he did it! He hit the ball and it went high in the air. Then Ben heard, "Run, Run, Run Ben!" Ben took off trying to run as fast as he could.

Sam the sneaker had to think fast. What should he do? Should he help Ben, or should he trip him? Should he allow his shoelace to untie? Should he put a pebble in his sneaker and slow Ben down?

"No," Sam thought. "No, No, No!" I can't do that. Ben *is* a nice boy. He *does* help me. He has been good to Sid and me."

All of a sudden Sam smiled.

He straightened his back, made sure his laces were tied tightly, made certain Ben's foot fit comfortably in his sneaker, and he worked as hard as he could to stay on Ben's feet and help him run.

He cried out, "Run. Run, Run Ben!" Run, Run, Run!

And Ben ran.

He ran as fast as he could, and Lo and behold:

He Hit a Home Run!

His team won, and Ben was thrilled! Loud cheering could be heard from the crowd. "Hooray!" yelled Sam; "Hooray!" yelled Sid, and they gleefully celebrated the victory with Ben and his friends.

At the end of the day, when it was time for
Ben to go to sleep. Ben thanked Sam and Sid.

"Thank you for helping me win the game!
You are the best sneakers I ever had!"

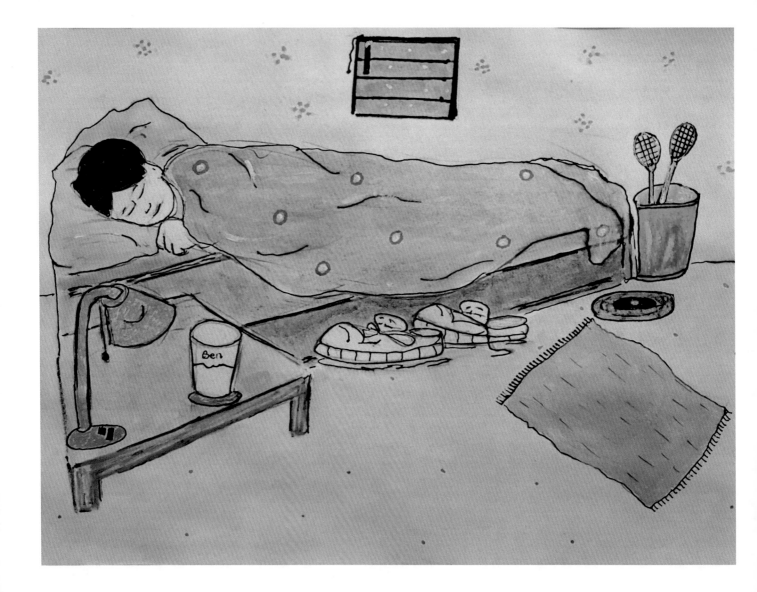

Sam smiled, and Sid smiled and felt
so proud. They closed their eyes
and fell into a deep sleep.

They dreamt of joyful people, smiling
faces and a beaming Ben, their newest
and dearest best friend.

After that day Sam cooperated and always helped Ben. He loved the fact that Ben was a part of his life. He felt like the grandest sneaker in the world!

He was Happy!

Made in United States
North Haven, CT
30 April 2024

51958720R00035